# Tales and Trails

## From The Storyteller's Garden, Grasmere

# With stories by
# Taffy Thomas
# the Storyteller

**Tales in Trust**

# Tales and Trails
## from the Storyteller's Garden, Grasmere

**Tales:** Taffy Thomas MBE

**Trails:** Martin Hanks

**Editor:** Helen Watts
www.astonhilleditorial.co.uk

**Book design and layout:**
Heather C. Sanneh

**Illustrations:** Steven Gregg

**Back cover photographs:**
Jon Yeomans

**Maps:** Martin Hanks

**Song, page 16:**
words by Mike O'Connor,
illustration by John Crane.

Printed and bound in Great
Britain by Xpedient Print
Services, UK
www.xpedientonline.co.uk

First published in Great Britain by

Tales in Trust, May 2013

**www.taffythomas.co.uk**

Tales in Trust,

The Northern Centre for Storytelling,

Church Stile Studio

Grasmere

Ambleside

Cumbria

LA22 9SW

**Tales in Trust** is part of the Northern Centre for Storytelling, a not-for-profit educational charitable company (company registration number 04473486).

A CIP catalogue record for this book is available from The British Library

**ISBN 978-0954106812**

**LOTTERY FUNDED**

**Tales and Trails** is part of a Heritage Lottery Fund project.

# Contents

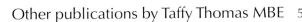

# Introduction

## The Storyteller's Garden

The Storyteller's Garden can be found at the centre of the Lake District village of Grasmere. Leased from the National Trust, it is run by the Northern Centre for Storytelling, a not-for-profit, educational, charitable company. All year round, the Northern Centre for Storytelling endeavours to attract a rich mixture of visitors and locals to the Storyteller's Garden through a variety of seasonal events which are, they say, 'for the young and for the young at heart'.

## Tales and Trails

This book is a part of a Heritage Lottery Fund supported project called 'Tales and Trails', undertaken by the Storyteller's Garden. For the project, the Artistic Director of the Northern Centre for Storytelling, Taffy Thomas, who was the first UK Laureate for Storytelling, devised five stories. Each story was site-specific to a recreational walk and either based on, or inspired by, the heritage of traditional oral storytelling. The heritage was not just the stories, but also the skills to tell them. Even more specifically, it was about sharing the skills to tell those stories, while taking groups of varying ages and abilities on the recommended walks.

In 2012, members of five community groups were tutored in practical workshop sessions and learned additional skills by participating in the walks themselves. The groups varied from schoolchildren and their teachers, Age UK volunteers and university student volunteers, to supporters of a local environmental project. With their training complete, the groups then took part in a special festival programme over the Queen's Diamond Jubilee weekend, which included all five 'Tales and Trails'.

This book, a unique collection of those five stories and routes, is a legacy of this innovative project for all the people who took part and for anyone wishing to take part and continue its heritage in future, whether they be Lakeland residents or visitors.

## Something for everyone

All of the trails in this collection start and finish at the Storyteller's Garden. The first of the stories – *The Fairy Boots* – is set in the garden itself. This allows

The King of the Birds is brought to life high up on Helm Crag.

The Dragon of Rydal Cave is retold with the accompaniment of a young violin player.

The 'Tales and Trails' project involved giving members of various community groups some new storytelling skills which they could then put into practice on the story walks.

The Hunchback and the Swan is shared on the shores of Grasmere lake.

for any participants who, for reasons of age or infirmity, are unable to cope with even a moderate walk. In fact, experience has shown that special needs groups value the garden as a safe space where they can sit, lie or even crawl on the grass while listening to the tale.

The Cat Fishers is a perfect tale for those who would like a gentle stroll, for wheelchair users, or for those with young children and pushchairs, as it is linked to a pleasant riverside walk and an easy circuit around Grasmere village.

For the more adventurous, there is a climb to the top of Helm Crag – the setting for The King of the Birds tale. Meanwhile for those wishing to go on a longer walk, The Dragon of Rydal Cave is set on the slopes of Loughrigg Fell and is complemented by a ramble to Rydal Cave and Rydal village which can be extended by a return walking route, or made easier by a picturesque bus ride back into Grasmere. Finally, there is a relatively easy walk to the shores of Grasmere lake – the perfect spot to share The Hunchback and the Swan.

## Cumbria's storytelling heritage

The five tales within this book are part of a huge storytelling heritage. Whenever you read or tell them, standing behind you will be the ghosts of all who have told them before. But also, within them, is the spirit of the inspirational Cumbrian landscape around Grasmere. The stories and legends have evolved from the people inhabiting that landscape, from the Pagan beliefs that surrounded the tales brought by the Norsemen – which existed around these parts longer than most other places because of the remote terrain – to the many legends brought by the missionaries and the invaders who arrived later.

By marrying up these five tales with walking trails, along which you can see for yourself the landscape and the locations which feature within them, it is hoped that the stories will become more accessible and even more enjoyable. By taking the reader to the very places in which the stories are set, this collection aims to bring you closer to the character and the spirit of the people whose heritage created them, and above all, closer to the character and the spirit of Lakeland.

**Taffy Thomas MBE** trained as a Literature and Drama teacher at Dudley College of Education and taught for several years in Wolverhampton. He founded and directed the legendary folk theatre company, Magic Lantern, illustrating traditional stories and songs with shadow puppets and circus skills. Taffy also founded and directed the rural community arts company, Charivari, with its popular touring unit, the Fabulous Salami Brothers, and fronted and performed in this company until he was sidelined by a stroke, aged just 36. He turned back to storytelling as self-imposed speech therapy.

Today, Taffy has a repertoire of more than 300 stories and tales collected mainly from traditional oral sources, and is now the most experienced English storyteller, having pioneered many storytelling residencies and appeared at the National Storytelling Festival in the USA and the Bergen Arts Festival in Norway.

In the 2001 New Year Honours List, he was awarded the MBE for services to storytelling and charity and, in the

# *Taffy Thomas MBE*

same year, performed for the Blue Peter Prom at the Royal Albert Hall. In October 2009, Taffy accepted the honorary, two-year post of the first Laureate for Storytelling, which saw him travelling the length and breadth of the UK, performing and running storytelling workshops in a wide range of venues – from schools and libraries to care homes and corporate offices.

Nearly all of Taffy's performances involve the storyteller donning his special Tale Coat – a unique, working piece of textile art. Covering this full-length garment are embroidered and painted images, each a trigger to a story in Taffy's repertoire. The moment Taffy puts on the Tale Coat, his performance becomes interactive, and members of the audience are invited to choose an image – and thereby a story – from this elaborate storytelling jukebox.

Taffy is a patron of the Society for Storytelling and as Artistic Director of

Tales in Trust, the Northern Centre for Storytelling in Grasmere, he holds events all year round in the Storyteller's Garden.

Taffy continues to tour nationally and internationally, working in both entertainment and education.

Nearly all of Taffy's performances involve the Tale Coat – a unique, working piece of art created by textile artist Paddy Killer.

For more information about Taffy Thomas, visit *www.taffythomas.co.uk*. For details of Taffy's publications, go to page 50.

Photograph © Steven Barber Photography Ltd/www.stevebarberphoto.co.uk

# One

Victorians lumped all folktales together as fairytales, but to me fairytales are stories about the Little People. This story was given to me by my mentor, Duncan Williamson and it was strangely appropriate that I was telling it in a school above the Rhonda Valley when the secretary brought me the sad news that the 79-year-old Scots Traveller had passed away. It is a story that children love to retell and the line about the cow saying poo instead of moo was gifted back to me on such a re-telling. Thanks kids!

# The Fairy Boots

Long before the Storyteller's Garden was created, the patch of land at Church Stile in Grasmere was a jungle where the grass grew long and plants grew wild.

One day, a tramp man, a gentleman of the road who had walked for many days without stopping for a meal, a sleep or even a wash, was walking out of Grasmere and was passing by this patch of unkempt land.

His feet were killing him, so when he spotted a particularly large tuft of grass, his first thought was that it would be a nice place to take the weight off his feet and have forty winks. He sat down and, because he hadn't stopped walking for so long, he kicked off his boots and was soon fast asleep.

The tramp had been so eager to sit down that he hadn't noticed that he was in the middle of a circle of toadstools: a fairy ring. And because he hadn't stopped for a wash, he hadn't shaved either so he had a stubbly chin.

After a few moments he was awakened by somebody pulling on one of his whiskers as though it were a tug-of-war rope. "OUCH!" he cried. He opened his eyes to discover that it was a tiny man in a yellow and green suit. "Get out!" yelped the tramp.

"Get out yourself!" replied the fairy. "You're in my place."

"What do you mean, I'm in your place?" asked the tramp.

"This is the fairy ring and my king, the King of the Fairies, it's his birthday today. We're going to have a party right here. You're sitting where the band is going, and where your old boots are, that's where the food and drink are going. In short, you're in the way. Clear off!"

The tramp looked down at his worn old boots and saw that the tops had come away from the bottoms. A thought popped into his head and he said, "If you would only give me some new boots, then I'll clear off."

In a twink, the little man was gone.

After what may have been a second, or may have been a minute, the fairy returned, clutching a pair of bright yellow boots in his fingers. He popped them down by the tramp and said, "There are your new boots. Now clear off."

The tramp picked the boots up and examined them. He saw that they were buttercup yellow and every stitch was perfect, but they were only half the size of one of the tramp's thumbs.

Angrily, the tramp complained. "Those boots are so small, they wouldn't even fit on my big toe." To which the little man replied, "Try them. Those boots are fairy boots. They're bigger on the inside than they are on the outside."

The tramp slipped one of the boots over his right big toe and the other over his left and, sure enough, his feet slipped right inside. The boots were a perfect fit.

Excited, he turned to the fairy. "These boots are fantastic!" he cried. "Where can I buy boots like these?"

The little man replied, "Money wouldn't buy you boots like that. However, my king, the King of the Fairies, tells me you can have those boots if you make me a promise."

The tramp nodded eagerly, so the fairy continued. "You must promise me that you will never ever tell a soul who gave them to you. And if you do, the boots will disappear back to where they came from at the speed of light."

The tramp promised and, doing up the laces, set off towards the road.

"Oy!" The little man called him back. "You've forgotten something. You've forgotten your old boots."

"But I don't need them any more," said the tramp man.

"Never mind that," said the fairy. "If you're in beautiful Lakeland, you can't leave rubbish lying around. Put the old boots in a bin or take them home with you."

The tramp picked up the old boots and put one in each of his jacket pockets, and it was a good job that he did.

He set off down the road, walking faster and farther than he had ever done before.

He didn't stop to eat, he didn't stop to drink, and he didn't stop to rest, even though it was hot midsummer. Nor did he stop to wash his feet and change his socks, so before long his feet started to smell. In fact, his feet ponged so badly that all of the cows looking over the hedge said 'poo' instead of 'moo'.

Now that tramp was more than two metres tall, so you can see how far his nose was away from his socks. But soon, even *he* couldn't stand the stench any longer. He was going to *have* to wash his feet.

The tramp looked into the next field and saw a fisherman standing waist-deep in a river, fly-fishing. The tramp thought that the fisherman would not be pleased if he muddied the stream, but too bad. He couldn't stand the smell any longer.

He walked over to the river, sat down on the bank and removed his buttercup yellow boots, putting them on a stone. (His socks were so rotten that they simply fell off.)

The tramp dipped his toes in the water. It felt so good that he couldn't resist standing up and swishing his feet around. But this made the stream muddy.

The fisherman turned to tell the tramp to push off, but then he spotted the bright yellow boots sitting on the stone.

"Those boots are fantastic!" he said. "Where can I get boots like that?"

The tramp replied, as the fairy had, that money could not buy boots like that.

"Well, whose are they?" asked the fisherman.

"They're mine," said the tramp.

"But they're too small," said the fisherman. "They can't be yours."

"Ah," said the tramp. "Those boots are bigger on the inside than they are on the outside."

"Where did you get them?" the fisherman enquired again.

"I'm not saying," said the tramp.

The fisherman told the tramp that if he couldn't reveal the origin of the boots, then he would have to assume that he had stolen them.

The tramp told the fisherman that he could assume whatever he liked, but he had certainly not stolen anything.

Then the fisherman announced that if the tramp would say where he had got the boots, he would leave him in peace. So, just to get the fisherman out of his hair, the tramp man told him the story of how he had come by the boots.

When he had finished his tale, the tramp looked up at the sky and realised that there was just enough daylight for him to walk another five miles. So he paddled back to the bank and bent down to put on his boots. But although he searched under the stones and in the grass, he couldn't find them anywhere. The buttercup yellow boots had gone back to where they had come from.

All the tramp could do was take his old boots out of his jacket pocket and wrap a piece of orange baler twine around them. Then he walked off down the road.

So, if you're in the Lake District and you spot a gentleman of the road wearing old boots with orange twine wrapped around them, then you know, as I know, that he once had a pair of buttercup yellow boots but he lost them because he didn't know how to keep a promise to the fairies.

# In the Storyteller's Garden

*Where the story magic begins*

Taffy Thomas in the Storyteller's Garden

The tale of The Fairy Boots *begins in* the Storyteller's Garden, *where many people say that magical things can happen (and where a circle of toadstools does, occasionally, appear). The garden is safe and appropriate for all ages and abilities. After visiting the garden, you can take the short and easy path through the churchyard opposite, to the bridge over the River Rothay. As you look downstream, it is easy to picture where the fly-fisherman might have stood, and where the tramp could have sat down to remove his boots.*

**Location:** The Storyteller's Garden, Tales in Trust, Church Stile Studio, Grasmere, LA22 9SW.

**Opening times:** The garden is a National Trust property and is a unique venue where family storytelling performances take place seasonally, usually on Bank Holidays, or by arrangement for groups. For an up-to-date list of garden events, visit *www.taffythomas.co.uk* and click on *Garden Events*. Alternatively, you can write to Tales in Trust at the address above, telephone 015394 35641 or email *info@taffythomas.co.uk*.

**Nearby car parks:** Red Bank Road, Broadgate Meadow, Stock Lane.

The Storyteller's Garden
has a secret I confide.
It's larger on the inside
than upon the outside.
It may look small but its true size
has not been measured yet.
For there's no limit to the troubles
you can just forget...

In the Storyteller's Garden,
always on the go,
words begin to grow.
In the Storyteller's Garden,
dear old Taffy Tee
works for hours among the flowers
with tales for you and me.
Have a nice mythology holiday
free from care, if you dare.
Morning, noon and night
in the Storyteller's Garden,
dear old Taffy Tee
tells myths and fables,
turns the tables,
lets your mind
run free.

Song words © Mike O'Connor. Illustration © John Crane.

## Story magic:
## Author's anecdotes

I have always believed in the power of story telling – or story listening – to make people feel better. Perhaps this dates from the time when I drew on my own interest in storytelling to facilitate my recovery from a massive stroke at the age of 36. I occasionally encourage a volunteer from my audience to join me on stage and assist in the storytelling, although I have something of a reputation for not choosing my volunteers wisely or safely. In my days as a street theatre performer, I once managed to choose the one blind man in the audience to check out a blindfold.

However, occasionally my innocence or lack of sensitivity has a really positive result. Over the Jubilee 'Tales and Trails' weekend, a mother arrived back at the Storyteller's Garden from an exploratory walk in the village to discover her ten-year-old daughter sitting by my storyteller's chair wearing a crown and assisting in the telling of a story called The Princess, the Ogre and the Star Apple. After the

story, she came up and expressed her surprise, as the youngster was, she said, not only painfully shy but also an elective mute. The magic of the story and the garden had worked, and the whole family was completely happy. My only hope was that they moved forward with this memory.

Also on the 'Tales and Trails' weekend, returning with a group from the lake, we passed a flock of Herdwick Sheep so I halted the group in order to share the mathematical story of The Seventeen Sheep. In this telling, three of the men stepped forward as the three brothers from the story, to calculate some simple fractions. A woman looked slightly horrified as her husband volunteered as one of the three, but I proceeded with the tale and, despite her worries, he correctly answered the mathematical question. After the story, the woman quietly told me that she had worried as her husband suffered from dementia. However, he had come up trumps and the couple had an uplifting, positive and normal experience of the true magic of stories.

## Two

*The beautiful riverside walk in Grasmere is surfaced, quiet and accessible. The path follows the beck – actually the River Rothay, but beck is a good Viking word left here a thousand years ago. It has many wooden benches for short rests and several bridges which are perfect for games of Pooh-sticks. A meander along the river usually includes sightings of rabbits, Herdwick sheep and a rich miscellany of bird life, but if you look carefully, you may also spot two pussy-cats! My mentor Duncan Williamson gave me the bones of this tale, saying, 'I'll give you the bones of this story: you make of it what you will'.*

# The Cat Fishers

If you look over the bridge into the River Rothay at Grasmere, you might spot brown trout or sea trout. If you walk along the river bank, you may well come to an old barn. Now, that barn is the home of two pussycats. One of these cats is an old black cat, and he's a bit like me, because he's a storyteller. The other cat is a little white kitten. She's young and she's fast.

Every night, the old black cat and the little white kitten curl up in the hay in the barn, and the old black cat tells the little white kitten stories. Those stories are usually about how good the old black cat was when he was her age, because those are the kind of stories that parents and teachers tell.

The little white kitten got fed up with the old black cat boasting about how good he used to be. So one night, the kitten said, "I don't want a story tonight. We'll go straight to sleep."

The old black cat said that this was a pity, as tonight he was going to tell her how good he used to be at fishing. Then, in the

morning, he was planning to take her down to the river bank and teach her how to fish.

The kitten said he should skip the story but still give her the fishing lesson on the morrow.

The following morning, the two cats yawned, stretched and padded out of the barn and down to the river bank.

The black cat demonstrated that, to tickle a trout, the little white kitten should put her paw in the water with her claws out, and when the fish swam over her paw she should flick it out onto the bank.

He demonstrated this several times and then announced that she could fish in that spot. He, however, was going a bit farther downstream. He knew somewhere better to fish, but wasn't prepared to give away all his secrets at once.

Excited, the little white kitten approached the water's edge. She put her paw in the water with her claws out, and as soon as a fish swam over them, she triumphantly flicked it out on to the bank next to her. She was proud she had caught her first fish, because she was young and fast.

Downstream, the old black cat wasn't doing quite so well. He was older and slower. He put his paw in the water with his claws out, but when a fish swam over his paw, he was too slow and by the time he tried to flick it out on to the bank, the fish was away and safe under a stone.

Although he fished the whole of the morning and the afternoon, the old black cat couldn't catch anything; he was just too slow.

As the sun started to dip behind the fell, he gave up and went back to see how the little white kitten had fared. Seeing him coming up the bank, the kitten stood proudly over her catch and arched her back in a threatening manner. This was her first fish and she planned to savour it for supper.

She called to the old black cat, asking him how he had done. On hearing he had been unsuccessful because he was too old and slow, the kitten started to laugh. The old cat pointed out that one day she too would grow old, and anyway his lack

of success didn't matter because she had caught a fish and they could share it.

The kitten pointed out that it was her first fish and she had no plans to share it. So the old black cat reminded her that he had taught her how to catch it, and that every night he told her stories, so perhaps now *she* should share something. The kitten again stated she had no plans to share.

And so the argument began. The two cats howled, yowled and hissed at each other. They made such a row that they awoke old Daddy Fox in his den on the fell-side, for the fox hunts at night and sleeps during the day. He came down the fell-side to investigate.

As soon as he spotted the fish by the kitten, he licked his chops, for Daddy Fox liked to eat fish too. He complained that the cats had woken him up and asked what their problem was.

The old black cat explained that they were arguing about which cat should eat the fish for supper.

Daddy Fox offered to be the decider. First he asked who had caught the fish.

The little white kitten proudly stated that *she* had caught it and so it was hers. The black cat said that *he* had been her teacher and so deserved his share.

Daddy Fox realised the situation was more complex than it had first seemed, but he had a cunning plan to resolve the dispute. He pointed out that they had quarrelled for so long, the moon was out in the sky.

Now, we all know that cats sing to the moon. That is why Daddy Fox's idea was a singing competition: the two cats should sing to the moon, and whichever sang the best would be rewarded with the fish supper.

The old black cat boasted that this would be him, as he knew all the old arias and folk songs, and what the young kitten called music – pop and rock – was just a noise.

The two cats put their heads back, drew breath, and started to sing:

"MEEEEEOW, MEEEEEOW, MEEEEEEEEEEEEOW."

While they were concentrating on their musical skills, they failed to notice as Daddy Fox stuck out his paw and flicked the fish towards himself. He seized the fish and took it back to his den to feed his vixen and his cubs.

The two cats sang on for another half an hour:

"MEEEEEOW, MEEEEEOW, MEEEEEEEEEEEEOW".

When they stopped singing, they looked down but there was no sign of a fish … and no sign of the fox. All they could do was return to the barn and go to bed hungry.

That was one night when the old black cat didn't tell any stories at all.

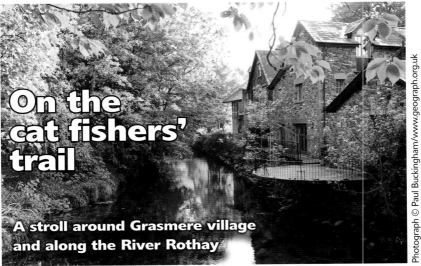

# On the cat fishers' trail

**A stroll around Grasmere village and along the River Rothay**

This short stroll takes you along the river bank where the old black cat and the little white kitten from our story went fishing, and past the barn which they called home.

The River Rothay, Grasmere village.

| | |
|---|---|
| **Starting point:** | The Storyteller's Garden, Church Stile, Grasmere, LA22 9SW. |
| **Approximate distance:** | 1.3 miles (2.1km). |
| **Difficulty:** | A flat, safe and accessible stroll that is pushchair and wheelchair friendly. Along the short stretches of road where there is no footpath, remember to walk on the right, facing oncoming traffic. |
| **Nearby car parks:** | Red Bank Road, Broadgate Meadow, Stock Lane. |

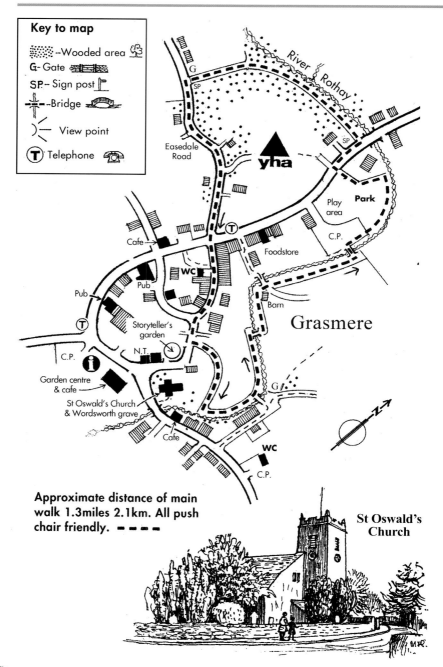

## Key to map

- 🌳 –Wooded area
- **G**- Gate
- **S.P.**- Sign post
- -Bridge
- )–(— View point
- (T) Telephone

Easedale
Road

River Rothay

G
SP

SP

yha

Play
area

**Park**

C.P.

Cafe →

Foodstore

**WC**

Pub

Pub

Barn

Pub

**Grasmere**

(T)

C.P.

Storyteller's
garden

N.T.

G

Garden centre
& cafe

St Oswald's Church
& Wordsworth grave

Cafe

**WC**

C.P.

**Approximate distance of main
walk 1.3miles 2.1km. All push
chair friendly.** ▬ ▬ ▬

**St Oswald's
Church**

24

## On the Cat Fishers' trail:

On leaving the Storyteller's Garden, cross the road and walk to the left, past Sarah Nelson's Grasmere Gingerbread shop. After a very short distance, turn right down a fenced path, signposted 'Riverside Walk'. Follow the path around the back of the churchyard to meet the River Rothay.

Follow the riverside path past the first footbridge, built to commemorate the Millennium, and then across a second footbridge.

Continue along the path, passing another bridge on the bend of the river. At this point, look out for an old barn near to a house on your right. Now converted, it was once the home of the two cats from *The Cat Fishers* story.

When you reach the next bridge, cross over the river again. Here the route turns right across the top of a car park.

Continue following the path at the side of the river, through a small park. On reaching a fence with a hedge, the path leads left to a gate onto the main road. Through the

gate, turn right and walk a short way up to the bridge, but do not cross it. Instead, take the signposted path, just before the bridge, on the left. (This short stretch of path is unmade so, if preferred, you can turn left out of the park towards the village and pick up the main route by the small green.)

The unmade path follows the side of the River Rothay for a short while before bearing left to enter a small wooded area. After this there is a narrow, fenced stretch.

The path ends at a gate onto a road. Turn left, going uphill for a short distance. Once round the bend, the road descends again, taking you past the entrance to a Youth Hostel on the left, before bringing you back into the village. Cross the main road and continue straight on where there is a small green on your right and a row of shops on the left.

Soon you will meet the main road again, with the large Wordsworth Hotel on your left. Go straight along this road towards the gingerbread shop. After a short distance you will see the Storyteller's Garden around the bend on your right.

# Three

*The bones of this story were given to me by one of my most generous storyteller friends, Illinois' Dan Keding. I have given it several different incarnations, but Rydal Cave was crying out for the story. Members of the Le Fleming family still live in Lakeland and their baronetcy still exists, although Rydal Hall has ceased to be a stately home. The rock by the cave entrance is still there though, and occasionally I persuade a small boy to sit on it and play a violin to accompany my story telling.*

# The Dragon of Rydal Cave

There was once a young boy who lived in the 'valley where rye was grown' – otherwise known as Rydal. His name was George, and he loved to play the violin. Not only that, but he also loved walking on Loughrigg Fell above Rydal Water and Grasmere Lake. Now along this route there is a deep, dark cave.

One day, George sat on a rock by the opening of the cave and he played a beautiful tune on his violin. At the end of the tune he heard a deep, silky voice which said, "Thank you for that music. For that I will tell you a story."

The voice of the creature – for George had no idea what it was – told a magical tale. At the end of the story, George said, "Thank you very much."

The voice asked George if he would return again the following day to share another tune and a tale. In fact, it asked, might George consider returning every day for a tune and a tale?

26

George promised that he would. And so it was, that the following day, George swapped another tune for a tale from the soft, mysterious voice.

By the third or fourth day, young George was beginning to wonder who or what his new friend was.

As the sun dipped down in the sky, a shaft of sunlight shone into the mouth of the cave.

Bravely, George stepped just inside the opening and looked down. He saw an enormous, green, scaly foot.

Looking up, he saw two shining golden discs. He was looking straight into the eyes of a dragon!

George said, "So it's you who has been telling me stories."

25

The dragon laughed, "Aren't you afraid of me?"

"Why should I be afraid of you?" replied George. "I play you music and you tell me stories, and we are friends."

The dragon said, "But I could crush you with one stamp of my foot, or I could fry you with one puff of my breath."

Now it was George's turn to laugh. "You wouldn't do that. We're friends."

This made the dragon very happy. He pleaded with George: "Please, promise you'll come and visit every day or I will be lonely."

George replied, "If you're lonely why don't you come home with me and live in my village?"

"I couldn't possibly do that," said the dragon. "Your people would kill me, because for years we have been at war. Ever since your great-great-great-great-great-grandfather George fought my great-great-great-great-great-grandfather dragon, we have not been able to be friends. Not until now."

Young George thought hard about this, and then he came up with an idea. He knew that the people of Rydal were worried. The crop had not been good and something had to be done.

So George said, "If we had a storyteller in Rydal, then visitors and poets would come to our village and it would be famous. So why don't you come and be our storyteller?"

George promised he would have a word with the Lord of the Manor, Le Fleming of Rydal Hall, and bring him to meet his dragon friend on the following day.

The dragon said, "Do you promise?" and young George, who knew the meaning of a promise, said, "Yes".

George went straight to the Le Fleming's house and told him about this new friend and his brilliant idea.

George told the Lord that he would take him to meet the storyteller, but that he would have to be blindfolded as the storyteller was very shy.

Le Fleming was astonished that there was such a thing as a shy storyteller!

The following day, the blindfolded Le Fleming put his hands on young George's shoulders, and his entourage of servants, also blindfolded, put their hands on the Lord's shoulders.

They walked all the way up to the cave and stepped inside.

George whispered into the darkness, "We've come."

The deep silky voice said, "You kept your promise," and started to cry with happiness.

As he did so, one great silver tear fell from the dragon's eyes and landed on Le Fleming's bald head. Feeling it drop, the Lord couldn't resist lifting his blindfold, and found himself gazing into the golden eyes of the dragon. The servants followed suit.

"Are YOU the storyteller?" asked Le Fleming in amazement.

So in his deep silky voice, the dragon told them a wonderful tale of a promise kept, and to George's delight, the grown-ups asked the dragon if he would come and live with them in their village, and be their storyteller.

The dragon said he would be delighted to do just that.

Then the Lord said, "Before you do, would you please grant us one wish?"

"And what would that be?" asked the dragon, to which the Lord of the Manor said, "Could we have a ride on your back?"

So George, the Lord of the Manor, and all the servants climbed on the dragon's back. The dragon spread his leathery wings and soared high up in the sky and circled above the beautiful lakes of Grasmere and Rydal.

Eventually, young George and the Lord whispered in the dragon's ear that they must return to Rydal as they had a promise to keep.

So the dragon landed safely down in the valley and his friends all went on their way.

The dragon lived happily in Rydal Cave for many years, going into the village every now and then to tell his stories.

Just as George had hoped, the storyteller attracted visitors and poets from far and wide and Rydal village became famous.

And when the dragon did die, he didn't die alone. He lay resting his head on the knee of a very old man called George, who had once been a little boy called George who had played him tunes in exchange for stories.

**Grasmere lake from boat hire jetty**

30

# Tales and Trails

**A circular route taking in Loughrigg Terrace and Rydal Cave, with stunning views over Grasmere and Rydal Water**

*Photograph © Dave Green/www.geograph.org.uk*

## In the dragon's steps

Looking out from the depths of Rydal Cave

This circular ramble leads you to the cave where young George met his dragon, and follows the route along which he led the blindfolded Lord Le Fleming. For a shorter walk, it is possible to catch a bus at Rydal Church, back into Grasmere village.

**Starting point:** The Storyteller's Garden, Church Stile, Grasmere LA22 9SW.

**Approximate distance:** Grasmere to Rydal: 3.4 miles (5.5km). Return walking route from Rydal to Grasmere: an additional 2 miles (3.2km). If taking the bus from Rydal Church back into Grasmere town, remember to check the bus timetables in advance.

**Difficulty:** A moderate ramble, mostly along level paths but with a brief climb up to Rydal Cave and later, on the extended return journey, a short climb up out of Rydal onto the Coffin Route. The walk takes you along some stretches of road where there is no footpath. For your safety, remember to walk on the right, facing oncoming traffic.

**Nearby car parks:** Red Bank Road; Broadgate Meadow, Stock Lane.

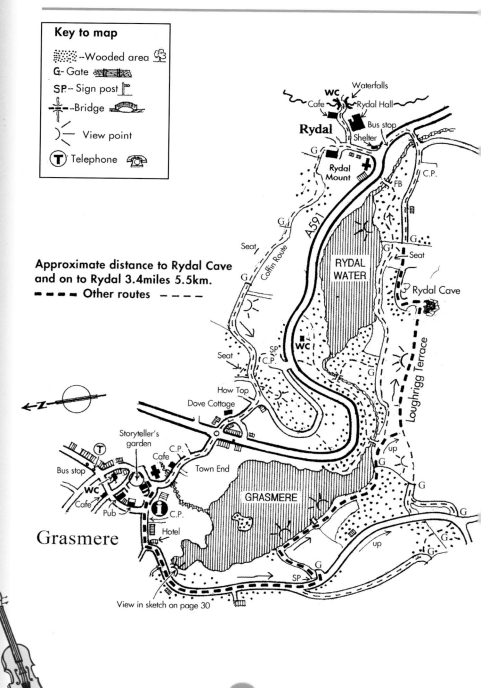

# Key to map

- ::::: --Wooded area 🌳
- G- Gate 🚧
- S.P.- Sign post 🚩
- ‡--Bridge 🌉
- )- View point
- (T) Telephone ☎

**Approximate distance to Rydal Cave
and on to Rydal 3.4miles 5.5km.**
**■ ■ ■ ■ Other routes  ─ ─ ─ ─**

Waterfalls
WC
Cafe
Rydal Hall
**Rydal**
Bus stop
Shelter
G
C.P.
Rydal
Mount
FB
G
A591
G
G
Seat
Seat
Coffin Route
**RYDAL
WATER**
G
Rydal Cave
Loughrigg Terrace
SP
WC
C.P.
G
Seat
How Top
Dove Cottage
up
G
Storyteller's
garden
C.P.
G
(T)
Cafe
Town End
Bus stop
WC
**GRASMERE**
G
Cafe
Pub
C.P.
up
G
**Grasmere**
Hotel
G
SP
G
View in sketch on page 30

## In the dragon's steps:

On leaving the Storyteller's Garden, turn right to pass the Garden Centre on your left. On reaching the road junction, head straight along the road, past an entrance to a car park on your left, towards the Langdales. On your right, looking north, there is a good view of Helm Crag, and soon after you have passed The Gold Rill Hotel on your left, Grasmere lake will come into view. Before long, you will pass a boat hire jetty and the views become shrouded by trees. Fortunately, this is not the case for long, as once round the bend, the road begins to climb gently and fine views of the lake re-appear on the left, while on your right you can see the hills of Silver How.

Continue on up the road. Soon after the small lane which forks off to the right, look for a signposted footpath on the left. Take this path through the gate and down to the lake shore. On reaching the lake, the path then turns right to follow the lake side, offering many fine views of the lake and the hills beyond.

Keep following the path, past an old boat house, and on through a wooded area, to a lake-side gate in a wall. After passing through, the path crosses a small beach, from which there are lovely views down the lake.

At the far end of the beach, at the top of the lake, is a footbridge. Here, bear right up the hill to join a main path onto Loughrigg Terrace. Where four paths meet by a walled wooded area, go straight on along the terrace rather than dropping down to the lake. The path is mainly flat with fine views of Rydal Water on the left.

At the end of the terrace, where the path goes into a wooded area, the impressive Rydal Cave comes into view on the right. The cave, which is the home of the dragon in our story, is well worth a visit if the pool at the entrance is not too deep, but care should be taken. In the past, rocks have been known to fall from the cave roof. Once a working quarry, the cave was a source of many of the roofing slates which can be seen on many homes and buildings nearby.

From the cave, the path follows the route which young George would have climbed up from his home in the Rydal valley. As you drop down in front of the cave, the path bends right, passing some smaller old mine workings. Soon you come to open ground where there are a number of seats, perfect for enjoying the view.

On reaching the main gate, zig-zag back on yourself to drop down to the lower path beside the lake. Go through the small gate on the right, close to the lake side, and walk through the woods. Soon you will reach a footbridge over the River Rothay. Cross the bridge and the main road, then turn right to pass the church and turn up the lane on the left. At this point there is a small shelter and, on the opposite side of the main road, is the stop for the bus back to Grasmere.

**To return on foot:**
Continue on up to the top of the lane. On the left is Rydal Mount with its attractive gardens. Now owned by the National Trust, this was the last home of poet William Wordsworth, who lived there from 1813 until his death in 1850. On your right is the driveway up to Rydal Hall, former home of the Le Fleming family and now a Church of England training centre and home to a small Christian community. The hall has attractive gardens and impressive waterfalls which are open and free to the public. In the gardens, just before the bridge over the head of the falls close to the Hall, there is a café and also some toilets.

After passing these two properties, look for the signposted path known as the Coffin Route – so named because this is the route along which the dead from Ambleside and Rydal were once carried for burial in Grasmere. The path takes you along the top of Rydal Mount then, once through the gate, it is hard to go wrong as there is only one clear path ahead. There are many fine views back across the lake to Loughrigg.

As you draw parallel with the end of the lake, your path joins a narrow lane to How Top and descends past Dove Cottage at Town End. A former inn, Dove Cottage was another of Wordsworth's homes. He lived here from 1799 to 1808 – the period in which he wrote many of his most famous poems. After Dove Cottage, cross the main road close to the mini roundabout and continue on into Grasmere. You will pass a car park and then a café on the right, before the road crosses the River Rothay. With the church on your right, the road then leads you round a bend to a right turn which brings you back to the Storyteller's Garden.

## Four

# The King of the Birds

*This tale is quite a chestnut, but like many such traditional, well or partially remembered stories, never fails to please. In telling, I usually reference the nearest high landmark – for example: in Lancashire, Pendle Hill; in London, Primrose Hill; and so on. Helm Crag in Grasmere, with its rock outcrops known as the Lion, the Lamb and the Old Lady playing the Organ, lends itself well to the tale, particularly as the one remaining Lakeland golden eagle has its nest on High Street on the slopes of Helvellyn, which is less than 5 miles from Helm Crag as the eagle flies.*

O ne day, the golden eagle was holding court, sitting in his favourite spot on top of the Lion's head up on Helm Crag. "Me, I'm the biggest. I'm the best. I'm the King of the birds. I'm definitely the best!" he cried.

He was a boaster and a poser. In fact, all the birds had grown fed up with him. He had got a bit too big for his beak! So they decided to bring him down a perch or two.

They went to see the wisest of the birds, who of course is the wise old owl, known as a *hulet* in Lakeland – as indeed it is in Shakespeare's plays. (A baby one's called a *yowlet*.)

They asked the hulet what to do, and the hulet said, "Well, it's obvious. Tomorrow, all the birds of the air must gather on the top of Helm Crag and when I say, '*On your marks. Get set. Go,*' you must all take off. Whichever bird can fly the highest is the King of the Birds."

When the birds told the eagle about the challenge, the eagle said, "Well, that's a waste of time. It'll be me. I'm the biggest and I'm the best."

The birds looked back at the hulet and said, "You see, there's the problem."

"Leave it to me," the hulet replied.

So the following morning, all the birds of the air gathered on the top of Helm Crag. The hawk posse gathered on top of the Lion. There on the Lion's head was the golden eagle, and there was the kestrel, the sparrowhawk, the falcon and the osprey. And as soon as they gathered there, the eagle started boasting: "What a waste of time! Me, I'm the biggest. I'm the best."

Perched on the rock known as the Lamb, right next to the hawks, were the big black birds: the rook, the raven, the jackdaw and the crow. And just a little bit farther along the crag, on top of the rock called the Organ, were the small birds: the robins, the blue tits, the great tits, the finches and a long line of sparrows.

Then a cacophony announced the arrival of the chattering magpies. They found a rock to land on, and were still chattering as they landed: *"One for sorrow, two for joy, three for a girl, four for a boy, five for silver, six for gold, seven for this story which has to be told."* (Incidentally, some say that the last line of this rhyme should be '*seven for a secret*', but you shouldn't tell secrets, whereas you *should* tell stories.)

As soon as all the birds had gathered there on the crag, the eagle started boasting again: "What a waste of time! Me, I'm the biggest. I'm the best."

And the hulet said, "Just a minute." He tiptoed along the line right to the end of the Organ, and there, on the pipe of the Organ, was the last to arrive, the smallest bird of all, the little Jenny wren. The hulet whispered something in the wren's ear. The wren just nodded then she turned and hopped all the way along the Organ and the Old Lady, hopped through the legs of the big black birds, and all the way round to the hawk posse. Then she climbed on the back of the golden eagle. She was so tiny that the eagle didn't feel the tickling as she nuzzled down in his feathers.

The hulet went back three steps and said, "On your marks. Get set. Go!"

They all took to the air until the sky above Grasmere was black with birds. Indeed, they cast a shadow over Ambleside which has remained to this day.

All the birds soared high in the air, but the big black birds shot up faster than the rest. They had found a thermal. It was early summer, and as the air hit the warm rocks of the fells, it heated up. And of course hot air rises, so that draught of hot air lifted the big black birds – the rook and the raven, the jackdaw and the crow and the hawks – until they were sailing up high above Helm Crag and Calf Crag, sailing high above the fells. As long as they stayed in that draught of warm air, they were fine.

But the small birds – the robin, the blue tits, the great tits, the finches and the sparrows – they started to tire. They drifted out of the warm air and hit the cooler air, and as soon as they hit the cooler air they started to come down.

They started to fall.

They started to descend.

And they landed back on the top of the Lamb, on the top of Helm Crag, back where they had started.

The next to come down were the magpies, still chattering: *"One for sorrow, two for joy, three for a girl, four for a boy, five for silver, six for gold, seven for this story which has to be told."*

They landed back on their rock and they looked up to the sky. There they could see the big, black birds, still riding the thermal, sailing gracefully above the mountains and above the fells. However, the smaller ones – the jackdaws – had started to tire. They drifted out of the warm air, hit the cooler air, and they started their descent. As they came down, they landed back on top of the Lamb, on the top of Helm Crag.

That just left the hawk posse high in the air, soaring up there as only hawks can.

But now it was the small hawks' turn to begin to tire – the falcon, the kestrel, the sparrowhawk, and even the osprey. They drifted sideways, and as soon as they hit the cooler air they dropped like stones. They came down and they landed back on top of the Lion.

Together, all the birds looked up and they could see just one speck remaining high in the sky, and they knew that the speck was the golden eagle. "Well, he might be a boaster and a poser, but he was right," they agreed. "He *is* the biggest. He *is* the best. He's still up there."

At that moment, the golden eagle also started to tire. Certain that he had proved his point, he just drifted sideways, hit some cooler air, and started to come down.

On his back, the little Jenny wren felt the change in altitude and, as the eagle started to come down, she launched herself upwards. So for that one wonderful moment, the wren was going up while the eagle was coming down.

The eagle landed back on the Lion's head. He turned and called out to all of the birds, even those perched on the Old Lady playing the Organ, "You see! I'm the biggest. I'm the best. I'm the King of the Birds!"

And all the birds said, "But there's still someone up there!"

The eagle looked up and sure enough, there was a tiny, tiny speck, high in the sky – the speck that you know was little Jenny wren. He let out a big gasp.

They all watched as the little Jenny wren drifted very slowly down and landed on top of the Old Lady's head, behind the Organ, then they all called across to her, "You see, Jenny wren! *You* are the King of the Birds, because although you are the smallest in size, you are the biggest in wit."

---

**The Wren Song**
*The wren, the wren is King of the Birds.*
*St Stephen's Day she was stuck in the furze.*
*Although she was little, her wit it was great.*
*If you boast like an eagle, you might share his fate.*

---

# Heading for a *bird's eye view*

**A rewarding climb to the summit of Helm Crag**

A hike of moderate distance but which involves a steep, rocky ascent to the summit of Helm Crag. At the top, you can search the outline of the rock formations for the Lion, the Lamb and the Old Lady playing the Organ. As the descent on the north side of the summit is very steep, it is avoided in this route, but experienced ramblers can follow a circular route along the path marked on the map which drops to Helmside, then back down the lane to rejoin the Easedale Road.

**Starting point:** The Storyteller's Garden, Church Stile, Grasmere LA22 9SW.

**Approximate distance:** Grasmere to Helm Crag and back: 3 miles (4.8km).

**Difficulty:** Although not a long distance, this walk involves a steep climb and some high rocky paths. It should only be made in good weather and by walkers who are well equipped, with suitably good footwear. The route involves some stretches of road where there is no footpath. For your safety, remember to walk on the right, facing oncoming traffic.

**Nearby car parks:** Red Bank Road; Broadgate Meadow, Stock Lane.

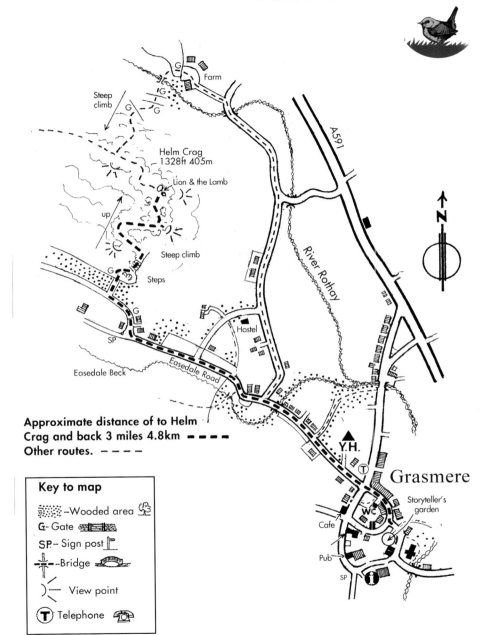

Farm

Steep climb

Helm Crag
1328ft 405m

Lion & the Lamb

up

Steep climb

Steps

G

SP

Easedale Beck

Easedale Road

Hostel

River Rothay

A591

N↑

**Approximate distance of to Helm Crag and back 3 miles 4.8km** ▬ ▬ ▬
**Other routes.** ─ ─ ─ ─

## Key to map

- ░░ –Wooded area 🌳
- G - Gate ▦
- S.P. – Sign post ⚑
- ✝ –Bridge 🌉
- )⚊ – View point
- Ⓣ Telephone ☎

Grasmere

Storyteller's garden

Cafe

Pub

WC

Y.H.

SP

**Heading for a bird's eye view:**
On leaving the Storyteller's Garden, cross the road and turn left to pass Sarah Nelson's Grasmere Gingerbread shop and then, further round the bend, the large Wordsworth Hotel on your right. Keeping to the right, take the narrow street ahead, with the self-catering apartments on your right.

On reaching the main road, where there is a small green on the left and a row of shops on the right, cross over and go straight ahead. This is Easedale Road. Continue along this road for close to one mile, all the way to the end. About half way along, the road crosses over Easedale Beck and, shortly after, a road branches off to the right. Ignore this and keep going straight on. After a bend in the road, and then a wooded area, the land opens up, revealing a view of the hills ahead and, in particular, Helm Crag.

At the point where the public road comes to an end, there is a group of houses and a signpost to Helm Crag pointing up an unmade lane. Go up the lane, through the gate, and soon afterwards, take the path that branches off to the right. Here, the climb up to Helm Crag really begins.

This well-defined path first zig-zags up around the edge of a disused quarry. A succession of steep steps then follows, running along a wall. This is a hard climb but the many fine views to be seen on the climb are good reward for your effort.

At the top, the path bears left, continuing to climb while zig-zagging onwards until the top of the crag is reached.

The summit of Helm Crag is at a height of 405m (1,328 feet), and if the weather is fine, this is a perfect place to share *The King of the Birds* story. You can also see if you can spot the rock formations mentioned in our story – the Lion, where the eagle and the hawk posse gathered; the Lamb, where the big black birds perched; and the Old Lady playing the Organ, where the small birds landed.

After enjoying the views from the summit, we recommend that you retrace your steps back down into Grasmere. However, for the more ambitious and experienced ramblers, there is a very steep route down the other side of the crag which leads you down to the River Rothay and to the farm at Helmside. From there, you can pick up the lane which crosses, and then runs parallel with, the River Rothay. Continue along the lane until it rejoins the Easedale Road just before it crosses Easedale Beck.

## Five

My mentor, the late Duncan Williamson, told me this tale belonged in England not in his native Scotland because the swans on his burns and lochs were not Mute, but Hooper swans, who merely over-nighted on Cumbrian lakes on their way home. Before he died at the age of 79, Duncan said that if you tell someone a story you never die – a completely believable form of immortality. Often, while telling this story on the lake shore, a pair of mute swans will fly in or swim up to me. If children ask, 'How did you do that?' I usually respond that the swans have merely arrived to hear their story.

# The Hunchback and the Swan

On the fell-side, near the lake in Grasmere, is a little thatched cottage. Many years ago in that cottage there lived a hunchback – an old man with a hump on his back; an old man so ugly that the people in the village would have nothing to do with him. Furthermore, the hunchback was completely mute.

But even though he didn't have any friends in the village, he did *have* friends: his friends were the animals of the forest. So sometimes, when he went collecting sticks, the hunchback was followed by a line of animals – the weasel, the rabbit, the badger, the fox and, flying overhead, the robin and the wren.

The hunchback also had one very special friend, and that was a swan who lived down on the lake. He so loved the swan that although he could not speak her name out loud, he called her his 'lady of the lake'. Sometimes the swan waddled after him and

he'd half turn and stroke her beautiful curved neck.

Now one winter, the hunchback disappeared. Was he alive or was he dead? The people in the village didn't care, but the animals cared because they weren't getting their breadcrumbs and their saucers of milk. So they went to find out.

Off went the line of animals – the weasel, the rabbit, the badger, the fox and, flying overhead, the robin and the wren – off up the lane towards the hunchback's cottage. They made a circle around the cottage as the robin fluttered up to the window to peep in. The hunchback was lying on the bed, completely still, and the robin whispered back to the other animals, "I think he may be dead!"

Just then, the robin tapped his little yellow beak three times on the window and the flicker of a smile spread across the hunchback's face. Excited, the robin reported back, "No, he's still alive but he's desperately sick."

The animals knew they needed help. They needed the help of the wisest of birds, the wise old owl, or to give it its Lakeland name, the *hulet*.

The robin flew off to the wood to where the hulet was perched on a branch. Settling next to the owl, the robin reported the details of the hunchback's sickness.

The hulet advised the robin that if the hunchback got a visit from his special friend, his 'lady of the lake', it may cure him.

Thanking the hulet, the robin flew off to the lake to where the swan was settled in her nest. Landing next to the swan, he told her of the hunchback's sickness, adding the owl's advice that a visit from her might be able to save the old man.

Immediately, the swan climbed from the nest and swam to the other bank. Then she started to waddle up the path towards the hunchback's cottage.

So there was the swan, followed by the line of animals – the weasel, the rabbit, the badger, the fox and, flying overhead, the robin and the wren. The animals formed a circle around the cottage – a magic circle.

As the swan waddled up to the back door and pushed it open with her yellow bill, the wren fluttered up to the window to peep in. The hunchback was still lying on the bed. His face was as white as the sheet he was lying on and he was completely motionless.

The wren whispered to the others, "It may be too late," followed by, "No, wait a minute. The lady of the lake is waddling over to the bed."

The swan tapped her yellow bill three times on the hunchback's forehead and he started to smile.

Excited, the wren reported, "We're in time! He's still alive!"

Just then, the swan tore some of the feathers from her left wing and jabbed them through the skin of the hunchback's left arm where they remained. Mystified, the wren reported this to the other animals. Then, the swan tore some of the feathers from her right wing and jabbed them through the skin of the hunchback's right arm, where again they stayed. Again, the wren reported what he had seen.

On hearing this, the circle of animals became very agitated and asked, "What's happening now?"

The wren reported that the hunchback had rolled over and the swan had torn some feathers from her back and jabbed them through the skin of the old man's back.

Inside the cottage, the swan then started to stroke the hunchback's hump with her yellow bill and, to the wren's amazement, the old man's back flattened out. Then, as the swan stroked the hunchback's neck with her bill, his neck became long and curved.

Everything had gone eerily quiet and the animals wondered what was happening. The wren informed them that they would just have to be patient and wait.

After some magical time, the back door of the cottage opened and, to the animals' amazement, out came not one but two swans. The swans waddled down to the lake, slid into the water and swam off side by side.

They say our friend the hunchback will be with his lady of the lake for ever now, because swans, like most waterfowl, only mate once in their lifetime, and when they do they mate for life!

However, strangely, since that day, most of the swans in the Lake District are mute ... just like the hunchback in our story.

# In search of *the 'lady of the lake'*

**A gentle walk to the shores of Grasmere lake – an idyllic location in which to share the story of *The Hunchback and the Swan***

Photograph © Mukumbura, 2011.

A mute swan on a misty south shore of Grasmere

*This is an easy return route to the lake from Grasmere village. However, if you wish to avoid retracing your steps completely, there are two other options: one producing a shorter route which loops around the other side of the lake; the other, a longer walk involving a circular section and a short climb up onto Loughrigg Terrace. As you stroll along the lake shore on any of the three routes, you may well be joined by the 'lady of the lake' from our story, in the form of a mute swan.*

**Starting point:** The Storyteller's Garden, Church Stile, Grasmere LA22 9SW.

**Approximate distance:** To Grasmere lake and back: 3.5 miles (5.6km). Lake circuit: 3 miles (4.8km). Longer, circular route via Loughrigg Terrace: 4 miles (6.4km).

**Difficulty:** An easy, mainly low-level, flat walk, suitable for most walkers but difficult in parts for pushchairs. At the top of the lake, the walk can be shortened or extended. Return route 3 involves a short climb. All three routes involve some stretches of road where there is no footpath. For your safety, remember to walk on the right, facing oncoming traffic.

**Nearby car parks:** Red Bank Road; Broadgate Meadow, Stock Lane.

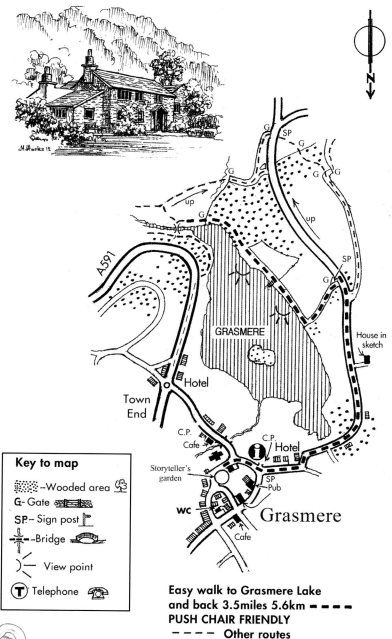

N

up

G SP G G
G G G
up
SP
G

A591

GRASMERE

House in sketch

Hotel

Town End

C.P. Cafe
C.P. Hotel
Storyteller's garden
SP Pub

wc

Grasmere

Cafe

## Key to map

- ▨ –Wooded area 🌳
- G- Gate ▦
- SP – Sign post 🚩
- ✚ –Bridge 🌉
- )⸻ View point
- (T) Telephone ☎

**Easy walk to Grasmere Lake and back 3.5miles 5.6km ▬ ▬ ▬ ▬ PUSH CHAIR FRIENDLY**
**▬ ▬ ▬ ▬ Other routes**

48

## In search of the 'lady of the lake':

On leaving the Storyteller's Garden, turn right to pass the Garden Centre on your left. At the road junction, keep heading straight along the road, past an entrance to a car park on your left.

On your right, looking north, there is a good view of Helm Crag, and soon after you have passed The Gold Rill Hotel on your left, Grasmere lake will come into view.

Before long, you will pass a boat hire jetty and the views become shrouded by trees. Fortunately, this is not the case for long, as once round the bend, the road begins to climb gently and fine views of the lake re-appear on the left, while on your right you can see the hills of Silver How. Also on your right, look out for the little cottage illustrated on the map which, although not thatched, is the inspiration for the hunchback's cottage in the story.

Continue on up the road. Soon after the small lane which forks off to the right, look out for a signposted path on the left, through a gate, which leads down to the lake shore. Take this path which, on reaching the lake, turns to follow the lake side, offering fine views of the lake and the hills beyond.

Keep following the path, past an old boat house and on into a wooded area, until it leads to a lake-side gate in a wall. After passing through, the land opens up, and the path crosses a beach, from which there are lovely views back down the lake. This is a perfect spot to read and share the story of *The Hunchback and the Swan*, and you may even find that you have some swans for company.

After taking in the view, you have three options for your return route.

## Return route 1

Retrace your steps, returning to Grasmere along the route you came.

## Return route 2

Continue along the beach to the far end at the top of the lake, where you will reach a footbridge. Cross the footbridge then turn left to follow the path through the woods beside the lake until it reaches the main road.

Turn left and walk along the road. After passing the large Daffodil Hotel at Town End, take the left fork at the mini roundabout and follow the road back into Grasmere. You will pass a car park and then a café on the right, before the road crosses the River Rothay. With the church on your right, the road then leads you round a bend to a right turn which brings you back to the Storyteller's Garden.

**Return route 3**

Continue along the beach to the far end at the top of the lake where there is a footbridge. Don't cross the bridge, but bear right up the hill. At the path junction at the corner of a wall around a wood, turn sharp right back on yourself to join Loughrigg Terrace. Follow this well-trodden path up the hill, with fine views of the lake now on your right. On reaching a gate, the path continues along a walled lane through woods to meet the road. Turn right down the road and follow it back into Grasmere, picking up your original outward route along the road.

## Other publications by Taffy Thomas MBE

**Books**
**Cumbrian Folk Tales** (The History Press, ISBN 97807524071273).
**Taffy's Coat Tales** (The Literacy Club, ISBN 9780956471604).
**Stories from the Storyteller's Garden** (Tales in Trust).
**Three Golden Apples** (Tales in Trust).
**Farmer Merryweather's Cow** (Tales in Trust).
**Telling Tales: Storytelling as Emotional Literacy** by Taffy Thomas and Steve Killick (Educational Printing Services, ISBN 9781905637287).
**The Linking of the Chain: Legends of the North** (Tales in Trust, ISBN 978-0954106805).

**CDs**
All available from Tales in Trust:
**Tales in Trust** (TTCD04).
**Take these Chains from My Heart** (TTCD06).
**Favourite Tales from the Tale Coat** (TTCD08).
**Stories from the Storyteller's Garden** (TTCD09).
**Ghosts** (TTCD10).
**Fairy Gold** (TTCD11).
**Legends of the North** (TTCD12).
**The Little Cobblestone Maker** (TTCD13).
**Tales for the Young and the Young at Heart** (TTCD14).
**Tell Someone a Story for Christmas** (Lyngham House Music, Lyng 218CD).

**Multimedia**
**The Gingerbread Man** compiled by Pie Corbett (Scholastic, ISBN 9781407100647). Children's book and CD for ages 4 to 7. Accompanying Storyteller teacher pack (ISBN 9781407100678).
**Dragonory** compiled by Pie Corbett (Scholastic Storyteller series, ISBN 9781407100654). Children's book and CD for ages 7 to 9. Accompanying Storyteller teacher pack (ISBN 9781407100685).
**The Boy and the Tiger** compiled by Pie Corbett (Scholastic Storyteller series, ISBN 9781407100661). Children's book and CD for ages 9 to 11. Accompanying Storyteller teacher pack (ISBN 9781407100692).

For details of all Tales in Trust publications, visit www.taffythomas.co.uk, email info@taffythomas.co.uk or write to: Tales in Trust, Church Stile Studio, Grasmere, Ambleside, LA22 9SW, UK.